Necco Sweethearts® MATH MAGIC

By Kris Hirschmann

SCHOLASTIC INC.

New York   Toronto   London   Auckland   Sydney
Mexico City   New Delhi   Hong Kong   Buenos Aires

ISBN 0-439-36538-4

Copyright © 2002 by New England Confectionery Company.
All rights reserved. Published by Scholastic Inc.
NECCO is a registered trademark of the New England Confectionery Company.
Sweethearts is a registered trademark of the
New England Confectionery Company.
SCHOLASTIC and associated logos are trademarks and/or registered
trademarks of Scholastic Inc.

12 11 10 9 8 7 6 5 4 3 2 1   2 3 4 5 6 7/0

Printed in the U.S.A.
First Scholastic printing, January 2002

INTRODUCTION

Math is always fun—but now it can also be sweet! You don't need real candy hearts to enjoy this book. Just follow the NECCO® Sweethearts® through page after page of colorful math problems, and you'll be a mathemagician in no time!

Math has never been this sweet before!

First, let's sort the hearts into groups according to color. Count the number of hearts in each group.

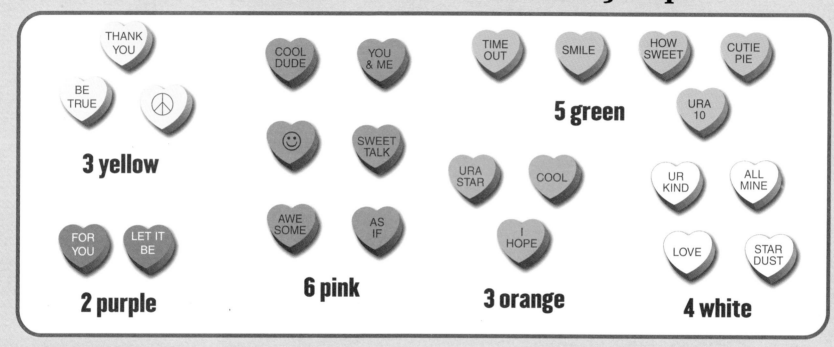

3 yellow

2 purple

6 pink

5 green

3 orange

4 white

How many hearts are there if you put the green and orange groups together?

5 + 3 = 8

Now let's look at it another way.

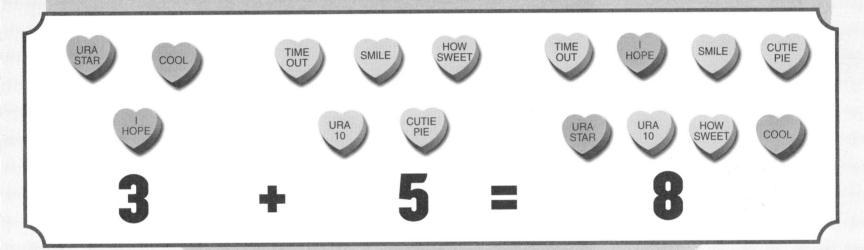

$$3 \quad + \quad 5 \quad = \quad 8$$

The total still equals 8.

What about up and down?

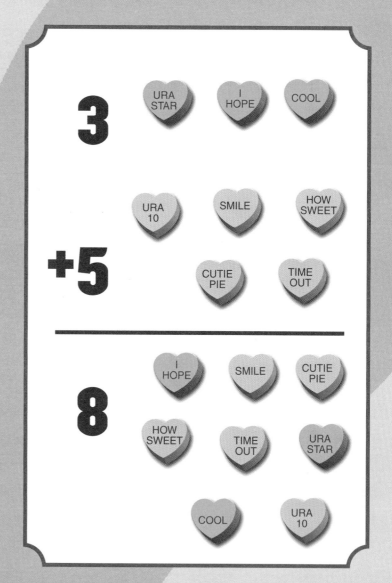

Now try one yourself. Add the purple and white groups.

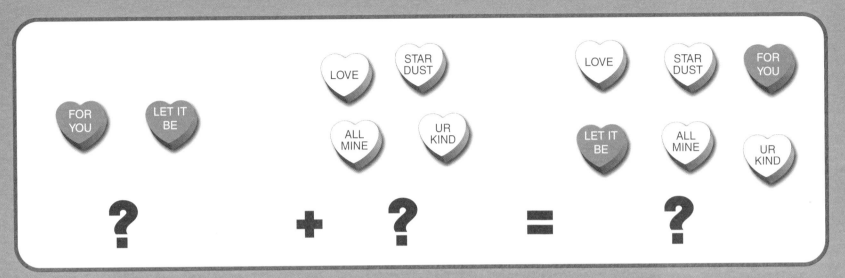

? + ? = ?

Add the pink and yellow groups.

? + ? = ?

Now let's sort the same hearts into three new groups:

- 3 hearts with 6 letters
- 5 hearts with 7 letters
- 4 hearts with 8 letters

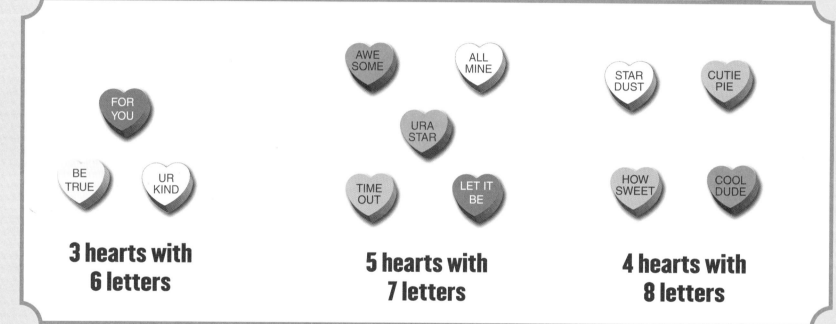

3 hearts with 6 letters

FOR YOU

BE TRUE

UR KIND

5 hearts with 7 letters

AWE SOME

ALL MINE

URA STAR

TIME OUT

LET IT BE

4 hearts with 8 letters

STAR DUST

CUTIE PIE

HOW SWEET

COOL DUDE

How many hearts are there if you put all the groups together?

$$3 + 5 + 4 = 12$$

Let's try another grouping activity.
Here we have one group of yellow hearts and one group of purple hearts.

Sweet Laughs

Why is the universe dirty?

Because it's full of

STAR DUST !

What happens if we move all the hearts with the letter S on them into the middle?

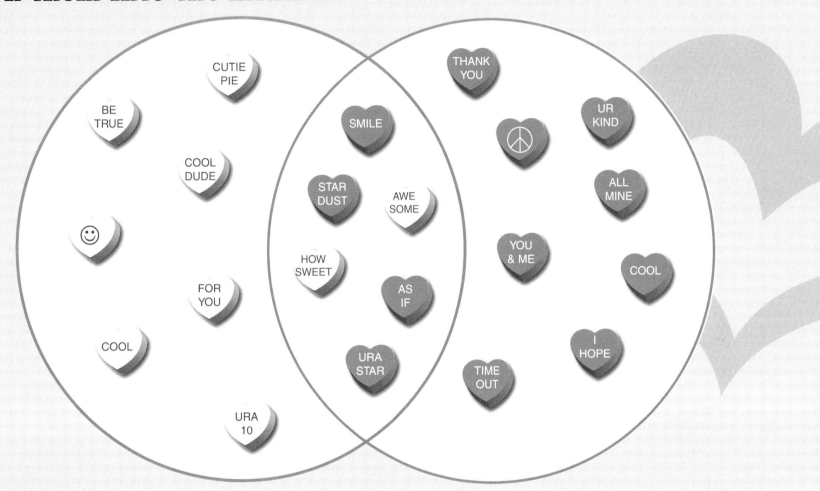

The hearts in the middle belong to two different groups. They belong to their color group, and also to the letter S group.

Look below. Each color heart is given a number. Each of these hearts belongs in one of the spaces on the next page. Solve the addition problems to figure out where each heart goes.

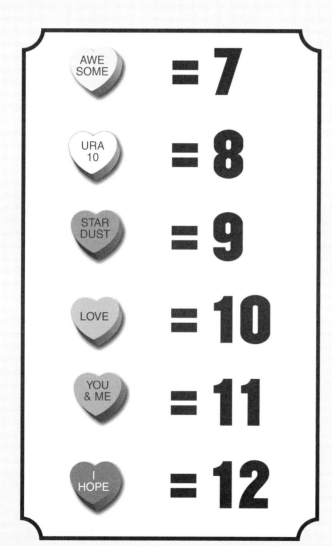

AWE SOME = **7**

URA 10 = **8**

STAR DUST = **9**

LOVE = **10**

YOU & ME = **11**

I HOPE = **12**

Sweet Laughs

The 7 saw the 1 and the 0 standing together. "My gosh!" she exclaimed. " URA 10 "!

4 + 5 =

8 + 3 =

3 + 4 =

1 + 9 =

5 + 7 =

6 + 2 =

Count the letters and symbols on each of the hearts below. You can use the totals to make addition problems, then try to solve each problem.

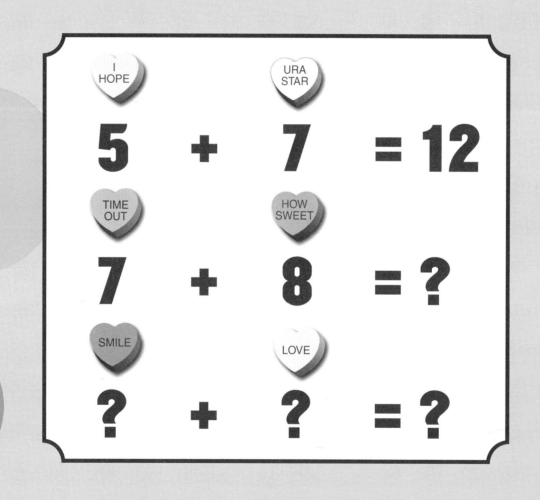

You can do it up and down, too!

$$1 + 4 = 5$$

$$8 + 6 = 14$$

Sweet Laughs

Why couldn't the snowman get warm no matter how hard he tried? Because he was always a **COOL DUDE**!

Answers: 8 + 4 = 12, 5 + 7 = 12

Now you can count up the number of letters on each heart and try these problems on your own.

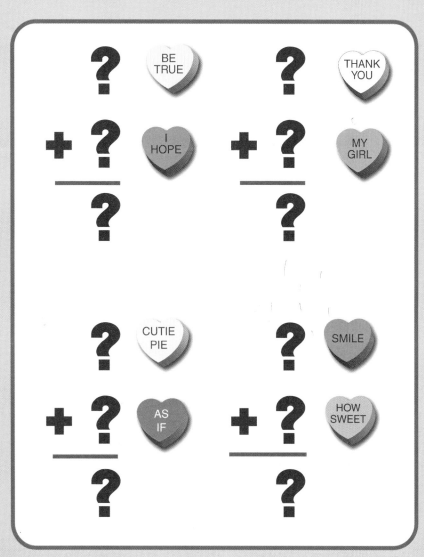

$$? + ? \over ?$$ BE TRUE / I HOPE

$$? + ? \over ?$$ THANK YOU / MY GIRL

$$? + ? \over ?$$ CUTIE PIE / AS IF

$$? + ? \over ?$$ SMILE / HOW SWEET

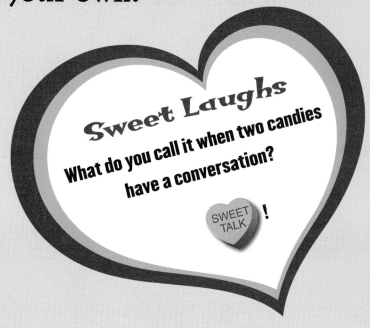

Sweet Laughs

What do you call it when two candies have a conversation?

SWEET TALK !

Make three big groups. How many hearts are there altogether?

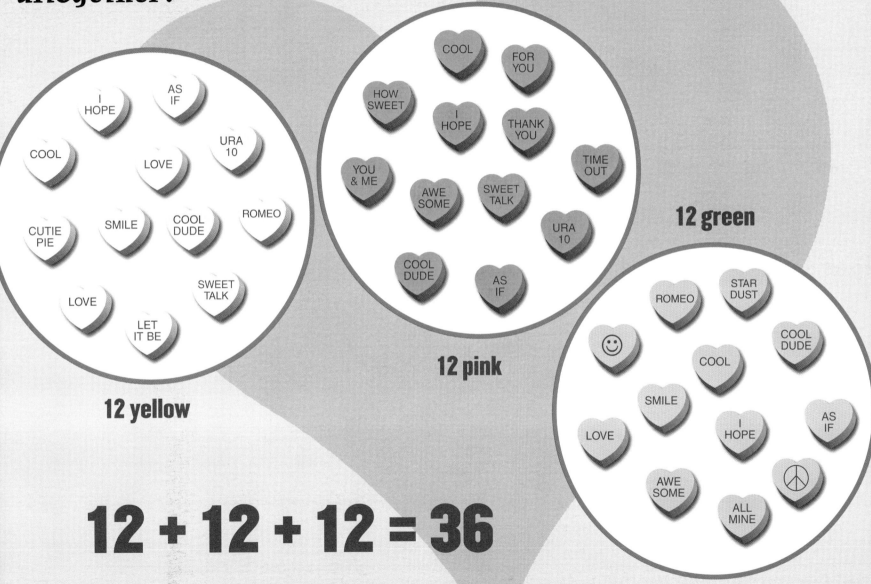

12 yellow

12 pink

12 green

12 + 12 + 12 = 36

Now let's try some multiplication.
It's easy if you know the rules.

4×3 means 4 groups of 3

Here are 4 groups of 3 hearts. How many hearts are there altogether?

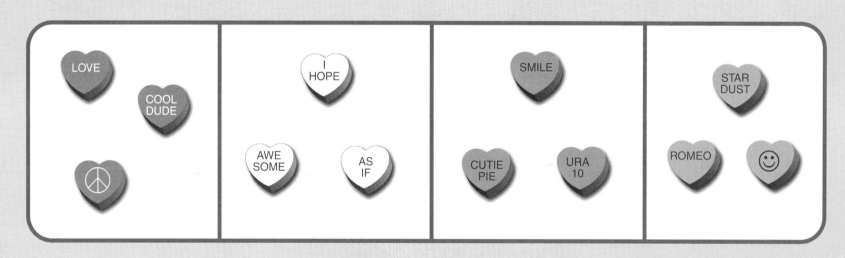

$4 \times 3 = 12$

If you reverse the numbers in the multiplication problem, the groups look different. But the answer is the same.

3 × 4 means 3 groups of 4

Here are 3 groups of 4 hearts. How many hearts are there altogether?

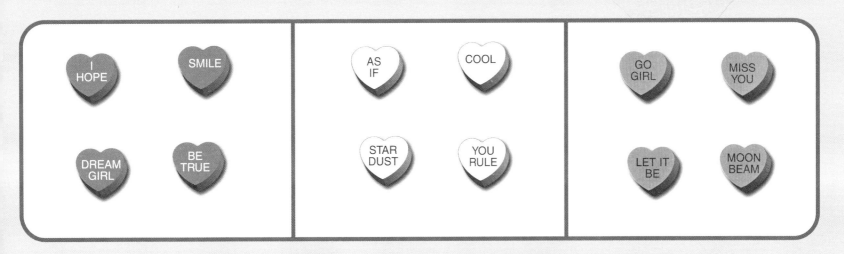

3 × 4 = 12

Now try it on your own. If there are 5 groups of 2 hearts, how many hearts are there altogether?

$$5 \times 2 = ?$$

Now let's look at 2 groups of 5 hearts. How many hearts are there altogether?

$$2 \times 5 = ?$$

Answers: 5 × 2 = 10, 2 × 5 = 10

Here's another multiplication problem.

7 hearts

2 ×  =

14 hearts

Sweet Laughs

What did the planet say to the sun?

URA STAR !

Try these problems yourself.

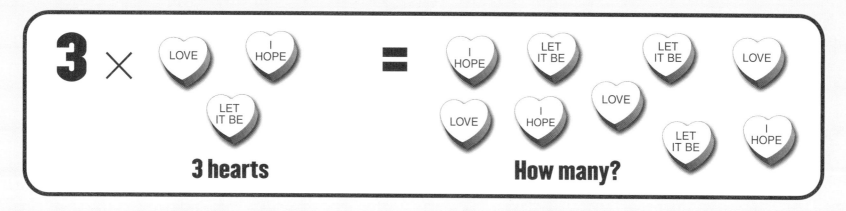

3 × [3 hearts] = **How many?**

3 hearts

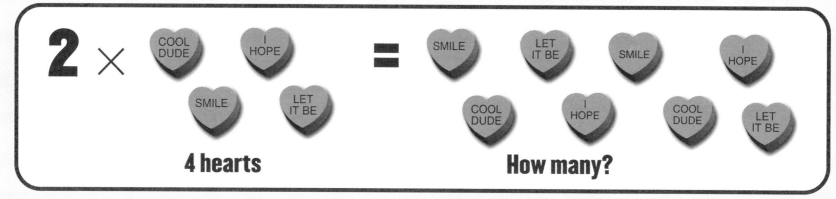

2 × [4 hearts] = **How many?**

4 hearts

6 × [2 hearts] = **How many?**

2 hearts

Answers: 3 × 3 = 9, 2 × 4 = 8, 6 × 2 = 12

Count the letters and symbols on each heart. Use the totals to make multiplication problems, then solve each problem.

$$1 \times 7 = 7$$

$$4 \times 4 = ?$$

$$? \times ? = ?$$

Sweet Laughs

What did the guard shout when the clock escaped from prison?

TIME OUT !

23

It's time to do some division! Look at this example problem.

8 ÷ 2 means split 8 things into 2 equal groups

Here are 8 hearts split into 2 equal groups.
How many hearts are there in each group?

8 ÷ 2 = 4

You don't get the same answer if you reverse a division problem. Let's try reversing the problem from the last page.

$$2 \div 8 = ?$$

Can you divide 2 whole hearts into 8 whole, equal groups?

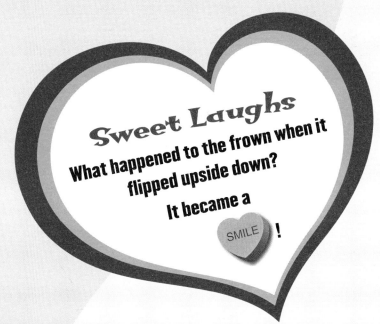

Sweet Laughs

What happened to the frown when it flipped upside down?

It became a SMILE!

No. You can't. 8 ÷ 2 is not the same as 2 ÷ 8.

Try it on your own.

Split 9 hearts into 3 equal groups. How many hearts should be in each box?

$$9 \div 3 = ?$$

Split 4 hearts into 4 equal groups. How many hearts should be in each box?

$$4 \div 4 = ?$$

Now try it this way.

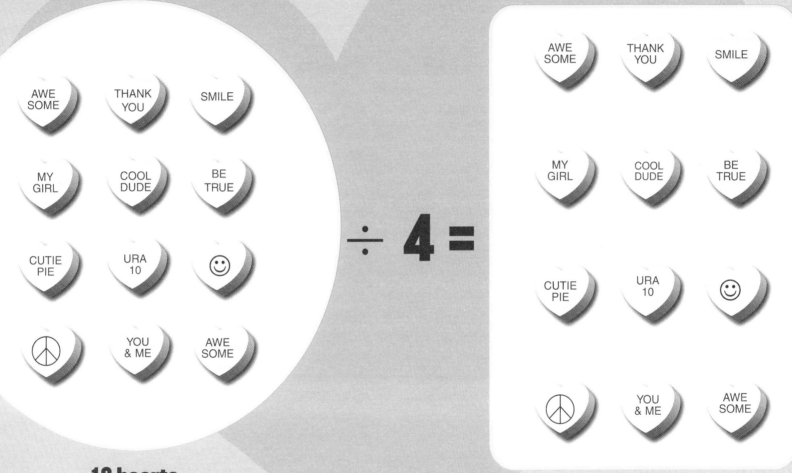

12 hearts

÷ 4 =

4 groups of 3

12 ÷ 4 = 3

Try doing these problems yourself.

Divide  **into 1 group:**

$3 \div 1 =$ How many in each group?

Divide  **into 2 groups:**

$4 \div 2 =$ How many in each group?

Divide  **into 3 groups:**

$6 \div 3 =$ How many in each group?

Answers: $3 \div 1 = 3$, $4 \div 2 = 2$, $6 \div 3 = 2$

Here is a bigger challenge! Can you split these hearts into 6 equal groups?

24 hearts

$$24 \div 6 = ?$$

Here is another number code where every heart is assigned a number. Each of these hearts belongs on one of the clouds on the next page. Can you solve the multiplication and division problems to figure out where each heart goes?

AWE SOME = 1

THANK YOU = 2

SMILE = 3

MY GIRL = 4

☮ = 5

YOU & ME = 6

Sweet Laughs

Miss Apple, Miss Pumpkin, and Miss Key Lime entered a beauty contest. What title were they trying to win?

CUTIE PIE !

5×1

$3 \div 3$

2×2

$6 \div 2$

3×2

$2 \div 1$

Answers: $3 \div 3 = 1$, $5 \times 1 = 5$, $2 \times 2 = 4$, $3 \times 2 = 6$, $6 \div 2 = 3$, $2 \div 1 = 2$

Congratulations, you're all done. Good job! Mmm . . . isn't math sweet?